Consultant

I love reading phonics has been created in consultation with language expert Abigail Steel. She has a background in teaching and teacher training and is a respected expert in the field of Synthetic Phonics. Abigail Steel is a regular contributor to educational publications. Her international education consultancy supports parents and teachers in the promotion of literacy skills.

Reading tips

This book focuses on cvccvc words
(c=consonant, v=vowel)

Tricky words in this book

Any words in bold do not sound exactly as they look
(don't fit the usual sound–letter rules) or are new and
have not yet been introduced.

> Tricky words in this book:
>
> **cowboy helper want to
> that star we the over
> give says me has**

Extra ways to have fun with this book

• After the reader has read the story, ask them questions
about what they have just read:

> *Name some of the things that the cowboy passed
> on his way to get the star?*
> *Where did the cowboy put the star once he caught it?*

• Make flashcards of the focus graphemes. Ask the
reader to say the sounds. This will help reinforce letter/
sound matches..

The cowboy
and I abolutely love
storybooks when we're
out on the range!

A pronunciation guide

This grid contains the sounds used in
the story and a guide on how to say them.

s as in sat	a as in ant	t as in tin	p as in pig
i as in ink	n as in net	c as in cat	e as in egg
h as hen	r as in rat	m as in mug	d as in dog
g as in get	o as in ox	u as in up	l as in log
f as in fan	b as in bag	j as in jug	v as in van
w as in wet	z as in zip	y as in yet	k as in kit
qu as in quick	x as in box	ff as in off	ll as in ball
ss as in kiss	zz as in buzz	ck as in duck	

Be careful not to add an 'uh' sound to 's', 't', 'p',
'c', 'h', 'r', 'm', 'd', 'g', 'l', 'f' and 'b'. For example,
say 'fff' not 'fuh' and 'sss' not 'suh'.

I am a **cowboy**!

Dog is my **helper**.

I **want to** get **that star!**

We gallop past **the** cactus.

We zip past the wigwam.

We puff past the ox.

We spot... a canyon!

Dog jumps **over** the canyon.

At last! I get the star.

I put it on my top.

We jump the canyon,
pass the ox,

the wigwam and the cactus!

A bandit!

"Quick! **Give me** that star,"
says the bandit.

But Dog **has** a plan.

"Duck!"

We get the bandit!

We get back to the campbed
with the star. I hug Dog.

OVER 48 TITLES IN SIX LEVELS
Abigail Steel recommends...

Other titles to enjoy from Level 1

I love reading phonics
Bad Rat
978-1-84898-277-2

I love reading phonics
The Best Gift
978-1-84898-396-0

I love reading phonics
Gran and Bret's Trip
978-1-84898-547-6

Some titles from Level 2

I love reading phonics
Wish Fish
978-1-84898-386-1

I love reading phonics
Chuck and Duck
978-1-84898-387-8

I love reading phonics
Pink Bunny
978-1-84898-550-6

I love reading phonics
Let's go to the Swings
978-1-84898-549-0

Some titles from Level 3

I love reading phonics
Bart's Go-Cart
978-1-84898-552-0

I love reading phonics
Queen Ella's Feet
978-1-84898-398-4

I love reading phonics
Puff Flies
978-1-84898-399-1

I love reading phonics
The Pop Duet
978-1-84898-551-3

An Hachette UK Company
www.hachette.co.uk

Copyright © Octopus Publishing Group Ltd 2012
First published in Great Britain in 2012 by TickTock, a division of Octopus Publishing Group Ltd,
Endeavour House, 189 Shaftesbury Avenue, London WC2H 8JY.
www.octopusbooks.co.uk

ISBN 978 1 84898 553 7

Printed and bound in China
10 9 8 7 6 5 4 3 2 1